The Secret Admirer

A Lunch Hour Love Story

Kristy K. James

Book Description

With the spark that used to burn so hot between them barely flickering, can Mark and Robin Pruitt reignite the flame before it's too late?

Mark never expected his marriage to become a casualty of the empty nest syndrome, but when their twins left for college, that seemed to be where it was headed. Unwilling to lose the only woman he's ever loved, he determines to save their relationship - he's just not sure how to go about it.

Robin has spent most of her life as a devoted full-time mother. Now that the girls are grown and out on their own, she realizes that she feels disconnected from her husband – and has for a long time. As she wonders about the future of their marriage, mysterious gifts begin to arrive in the mail.

Soon, it appears a stranger might mean her harm, and it doesn't take long before Robin begins to see her husband in a new light.

If you love a good clean and wholesome romance (with a little mystery thrown in) you just might love this Lunch Hour Love Story. Brought to you by the author of the popular Coach's Boys series, The Secret Admirer is sure to keep you turning the pages – all the way to its surprising end.

Dedication

To Kathie... Once again, thank you for making another book the best it can be!

Chapter 1

Robin Pruitt stood at the front door, waving like her last name was Clampett. Yeah. That was the one way to describe the flapping going on at the end of her arm. She didn't really care though. Those were her daughters and she was going to miss them like crazy.

In the distance, she could see Haley's sweet face as she looked over the seat blowing kiss after kiss. From the driver's side, Alexis waved out the window. Robin's motherly instinct kicked into high gear thinking about her bare skin exposed to the eleven degree windchill. Add in the twenty-five mile an hour speed limit and visions of frostbite started dancing in her head.

But her firstborn, headstrong daughter wouldn't think about something like that. Not anymore. Not without her there to remind her. Not since she and her sister turned eighteen last summer and were now considered adults. At least in the eyes of the world. To her, they were still her babies. They always would be.

And now that they'd all experienced the first round of being apart for months, saying goodbye had been a million times harder. Like hers, she knew their faces were streaked with tears. They'd fallen from eyes that had been too bright as they stood talking in the foyer, pretending life hadn't changed. Except it had and while they might not miss her quite as much as she missed them, miss her they would. It might be a busy, exciting time in their lives but she was still their mom.

Thank the good Lord for cell phones, email, texting, and Skype. At least they could visit long distance, as much as their crazy schedules allowed anyway. It wasn't the same as having them home but better than nothing.

She watched as they rounded the corner at the end of their road and then they were gone. It would be summer break before she got to hug them again, unless they found time to come back for an occasional weekend.

Robin sighed, wiping her cheeks as she closed the door against the cold, and the snow that had been falling since before the alarm had gone off at seven. Yet another thing to worry about, though the news stations claimed road conditions were still good. Thank goodness Allendale was only about ninety minutes away.

"Ninety minutes *too far* away," she muttered with a frown.

As the quiet in the house settled around her, she felt a restless stirring, a need to play every depressing song ever written. Except she wasn't one to wallow in sadness. Not if she could avoid it.

With a sigh, she walked to the living room, her steps slow, reluctant. A glaring reminder of the holiday that ended too soon, the tree stood in the corner, its decorations as festive as when they'd put it up on Thanksgiving. Bare of the gaily wrapped gifts though, it wasn't festive at all. Instead, it looked as lonely as she felt since what was left of her Christmas spirit had driven away with the girls.

Squaring her shoulders, she decided it was time to undecorate. She smiled a little at the term the girls had coined when they were four. If you could wrap and unwrap, do and undo, and braid and unbraid, you could decorate and undecorate. By the time they learned better, everyone was so used to saying it, it just stuck.

Robin sighed again. There was no point in putting it off in hopes it would get easier. It wouldn't. So it was best to just get it done and out of the way.

Hauling empty boxes from the closet beneath the open stairway, she found herself resenting her husband again. He'd taken off immediately after breakfast, three hours before Haley and Alexis were due to leave and hadn't bothered coming back. They all knew he had problems with goodbyes and that they should consider them said when he'd kissed each of their cheeks on his way out the door. Except he was their father. There was no excuse.

Then again, there was no excuse for a lot of the stuff that been happening since August. The empty-nester syndrome had hit them hard when the girls left for college and she wasn't sure their marriage would survive it. She wasn't even sure she wanted it to. Not anymore. Mark wasn't the same man she married twenty years ago and lately, she'd begun to wonder why they'd gotten together in the first place. If they'd ever had anything in common, it was gone now.

She tried to focus on the task at hand, noting that while the pine scent lingered, needles had begun to dry out. They poked and scratched her hands as she removed handfuls of tinsel and dozens of decorations.

Blinking back tears, she cradled the ones the girls had made in grade school. Popsicle stick stars from kindergarten. Paper plate and doily angels from third grade. They were starting to yellow around the edges a bit but still took center stage each holiday season, one on the top of the tree, the other on the mantle.

When it came time to remove the garland and lights, needles started falling so fast they reminded her of the snow piling up outside. She made a mental note to grab an old sheet to wrap the tree in before Mark hauled it to the road later. She should have put one on the floor but this had been their first Christmas with a real one and she hadn't expected it to start falling apart on her.

A new tradition for the new time in their lives, Haley had decided. Ha! Robin snapped a couple of photos of the mess. That way, when they came home next year to find the box with their old artificial tree parked in the middle of the living room, they'd know why.

By the time she'd packed away a dozen fat candles, the Nativity scene, and other decorations scattered throughout the house, her anger hadn't cooled by a single degree. It was fueled, she knew, by Mark's continued absence. As she taped the boxes up to prevent any dust—or spiders—from sneaking in, she wasn't sure she would be able to stop herself from ripping into him when he finally did show up.

The doorbell pealed as she carried the first box to the closet. With a sigh, she sat it back down and walked to the door. Through the peephole, she saw a delivery truck parked at the curb. A man sporting a hat with the logo for a local florist on it stood on the porch. He was holding a vase of flowers and looked as though he'd rather be anywhere but in the middle of a minor snowstorm.

What in the world?

"Good afternoon, ma'am," the young man said, smiling a quick smile before he glanced at the card tucked into a dozen red roses. When he looked back up at her, his brows rose. "Robin Pruitt?"

"That's me," she said, opening the storm door to take the cold glass vase he held out.

"Then these are for you. Happy belated Christmas," he told her, shaking his head when she asked him to wait a moment so she could get a tip. "It's already been taken care of. Have a great day!" And with that, he trotted back out to his truck.

Curious, Robin carried the vase to the kitchen, sat it on the counter, and took the tiny envelope from the plastic holder. Sliding the card out, she read,

I knew you'd be feeling a little blue today and hope these flowers might help to cheer you. As always you look beautiful today, sweetheart.

MARK PRUITT SAT IN his car, scrunched down behind the steering wheel like a peeping Tom. Only the top of his head, covered in a dark blue cap, poked above it, just far enough to see out the window. Watching as Alexis's red Jetta disappeared from sight, he felt tears sting his eyes.

Since they'd left three months ago to start their new lives as legal, independent adults, *his* life was falling apart. It was spiraling out of control like a tornado tearing through the county, destroying everything in its path. Only this one was destroying his marriage and he didn't know how to stop it.

When he'd taken his vows twenty years ago, he'd meant them. Back then, he'd never have believed he and Robin could drift so far apart they'd be living together like strangers. Like two people who had nothing more in common than the daughters they'd brought into the world on a warm summer day a little more than eighteen years ago.

Life had been perfect, the time flying by like there was a race to an invisible finish line no one bothered to tell him about. Now, he spent most of that time avoiding home because being alone with Robin was hard. Their conversations were stilted and uncomfortable. More often than not, when he went to bed, it was alone. She would sit up watching television or playing on the computer for hours. Their love life had dwindled to nothing and he didn't know what to do anymore.

After a few minutes, hoping in vain that the girls would turn around and come home, he started the car, driving aimlessly around town trying to kill time. Robin would be depressed because they were gone and he wouldn't know how to comfort her. Not that she'd let him try. She'd pretend she was fine, hiding the hurt and loneliness, the same as he would do.

There was a time when they'd have consoled each other, just like they'd done during the three weeks of camp each summer until the girls started high school. He and Robin had been best friends then and he missed that, missed *her*, but he couldn't seem to fix things. He hadn't even realized things were broken until Haley and Alexis moved out. Now, he needed a book, or someone, to tell him what to do to make his marriage right again.

And he needed to make it right because he couldn't stand the thought of living the rest of his life without her. Then again, he wasn't sure he could stand living like this either, afraid to go home because all that waited for him there was a stranger.

Everyone always said it took two to tango but somewhere along the way, he'd lost the ability to lead.

Eventually, well after lunch, he pulled into the garage. She'd be furious with him for cutting out this morning. Like a coward. Steeling himself for the cold shoulder and glare that were waiting for him, he opened the door to the kitchen. Except, to his surprise, Robin greeted him with a smile.

"They're beautiful," she said, her voice soft, almost like it used to be. "Thank you, Mark."

"For what?" he asked, his brows drawing together before his gaze landed on the vase sitting in the center of the table.

"These," she explained, looking at him like he should know what she was talking about. "The flowers."

Someone sent his wife flowers? And she thought they were from him?

"Robin, I can't tell you how much I wish I'd thought to do this," and he really did, "but I didn't send them."

He felt a little sick when she handed him the card. The words made it sound like they'd come from a husband. Or a boyfriend, or lover. Except for him though, she'd never been with anyone else. At least he hoped she hadn't because they'd been together since they were in the tenth grade.

She wasn't involved with anyone else though. She'd been too sincerely pleased, believing they were from him, for it to have been an act. That meant his wife had an admirer. He didn't like the thought. No, he didn't like it one bit.

Robin must not have either because after a few moments, moments she spent struggling to hide her disappointment, she got to her feet, emptied the vase of its water and threw it in the trash. Her pleasure gone, she seemed a little spooked. He didn't blame her. Whoever sent it said she looked beautiful which meant they must have seen her today. And the only people who had seen his wife had been him and their daughters.

"The girls," he said, a feeling of relief washing over him. "It had to have been the girls, Robin." He watched as she stood there trying to decide what to do. Mark thought she'd retrieve the flowers but she grabbed her phone off the counter instead.

"Hey Hailey, it's Mom. I just wanted to tell the two of you thanks for the flowers." From the look on her face, it was clear they hadn't come from them either. The unease returned, settling in his stomach like a rock.

He watched as they chatted a while longer. From her responses, Haley wanted to know what her mother was talking about and Robin tried to set her mind at ease. Apparently, it hadn't helped and their daughter's response made her even more nervous.

When she hung up, her face was pale. He wanted to wrap his arms around her, hold her close, and assure her she didn't need to worry. That he'd keep her safe. That he'd always keep her safe. But he didn't.

"Do you think we should call the police?" he finally asked, folding his arms across his chest to keep from reaching for her.

"I don't know. What are we going to say? Somebody sent me flowers? They'd probably laugh at us."

"Yeah. Probably. Maybe we should hold onto them though. Just in case."

He was starting to feel a little paranoid but was relieved when Robin snatched the vase out of the trash and carried it to the garage. He heard her sit it on a shelf with a thunk. Out of sight but probably not out of her mind. Not anymore than they were out of his.

Chapter 2

"Robin Pruitt, please come to the service desk," a voice over the intercom said, then repeated, "Robin Pruitt, please come to the service desk."

Her first reaction was to check her purse for her wallet. It was there, along with her phone and a few other items. So why would they be paging her? Had there been a contest she didn't remember entering? But even if there had been, how would they know she was in the store now?

The squeaky wheel on her cart serenaded her all the way to the front of the store and she stood in line behind three other customers, waiting her turn, still wondering what was going on. And hoping it was worth her time. All she'd had left on her shopping list were three more items, and then she could have checked out and headed home. She didn't hate shopping but she didn't love it either so she was always happy to get the trips over as quickly as possible.

"A little boy said he found this outside and brought it in to us," the service rep explained after she identified herself. "It has your name on it." She held out a small package with a card addressed to her.

Robin's hands were shaking as the woman placed the small package she didn't want in her hands. It couldn't have been a coincidence that she'd gotten the flowers the week before and now this. And if whoever was doing this knew she was in the store, then he'd obviously been following her. The thought scared her more than she wanted to admit.

Somehow, she forced herself to collect the remaining things on her list, check out, and get to the car, glancing all around with every step. If any of the other shoppers saw her, they'd probably laugh at how silly she looked. But if the guy was still here, still following her, she wasn't going to be caught by surprise.

In record time, she loaded the bags in the trunk of the car, climbed in the driver's seat, and locked the doors with the push of a button. She tried to take a few deep, calming breaths. Instead, she breathed too fast and wound up feeling a little dizzy. She leaned her head against the cold steering wheel to wait until the feeling passed. A light rap against the window scared her enough that she screamed.

"Oh my word," Robin breathed, looking up to see one of her elderly neighbors beside the car. She was shaking harder now but managed to get the key in the ignition and turned enough so she could roll the window down a bit. "I'm sorry, Mrs. O'Brien. You startled me."

"Then I need to apologize. I just saw you in the store and thought you were looking a little pale. And then I saw you here and thought I should make sure you're all right."

"Oh, I'm fine," she lied, hoping her laugh didn't sound as fake to Mrs. O'Brien as it did to her. "I forgot to eat."

"Blood sugar a little low?"

"Yeah, I imagine it probably is. Lunch is the first thing I'm going to see about as soon as I get home." It wasn't, but it seemed to satisfy the other woman who stared at her for a moment, then nodded.

"Will you be able to drive?"

"Oh sure. I'm feeling better already." And she was. Just having someone nearby that she knew made her feel a little safer, even if that person was a frail old woman who had to be pushing eighty.

"Well, I'll follow you as far as your house to make sure. Give me two minutes. I'm parked just over there."

"Thanks. I appreciate it."

Not until she was in the house, the groceries on the counter, the door securely locked, did Robin decide to open the package. Maybe she had it all wrong. Maybe it was a coincidence and it wasn't from whoever sent the flowers. She stood near the sink and removed the small envelope.

Dear Robin, I hope you enjoyed the flowers and thought of me often. Maybe this movie will show you exactly what you mean to me.

Her breath caught in her throat when she pulled out a VCR tape of an early nineties movie. She and Mark had watched it at the theater shortly after its release. An abusive husband, obsessed with his wife, hunted her down after she managed to escape from him. Robin remembered it as being suspenseful and scary and she'd been glad she'd married a man like Mark. Even though they had been growing apart the past few years, he was still better than the guy in the movie had been. Better than the guy who was sending her this stuff.

"Mark?" she said, her voice barely above a whisper when he answered his phone at work.

"Robin?" She could hear the immediate concern in his voice. "What's happened?"

"He sent another gift."

"I'll be right home."

ENOUGH WAS ENOUGH, Mark thought, wishing he could find whoever was sending his wife gifts and beat him to within an inch of his life. When he'd arrived home, Robin had been pale, wiping down counters and polishing appliances that didn't need cleaning. That's what she'd always done when she was stressed or upset. Cleaned house.

He didn't blame her for being upset about the movie. Like her, he remembered it and in his mind, felt it was some sort of threat. But she still didn't want to phone the police so it joined the flowers in the garage. In the two days since she'd received it, she'd been acting like it hadn't happened. Mark, on the other hand, spent those days installing better deadbolts on the exterior doors and security locks on all of their windows. Robin could pretend all she wanted but keeping her safe was his top priority.

A little good had come from it though. He was spending every moment he wasn't working at home and she'd been finding excuses to be wherever he was, like she was afraid to be alone. And she probably was.

He'd suggested maybe going to the Humane Society to get a dog but it seemed she wasn't quite that scared. She'd always been a little nervous around dogs so they'd never gotten a pet, not even when the girls were younger and had begged and pleaded for a golden retriever. It was the safest, most easy going dog ever born, they'd argued, to no avail. They hadn't been able to persuade their mother.

"Ready for some coffee?" Robin asked, coming up behind him, her hands wrapped around a steaming mug. He noted that she'd added cream to it. She always drank hers black. He always made his light and sweet.

"Sure. Thanks." He smiled at her as she handed it over, her fingers brushing against his for the briefest of moments. Mark felt the same jolt of desire at her touch as always and wished again that he knew how to fix whatever had gone wrong.

"I've got some pizza crust going in the bread machine," she said after an awkward silence. "And I made a batch of sauce. I—thought we might make an everything-but-the-kitchen-sink pizza. Like we used to. If that's okay with you."

He watched her cheeks turn a pretty shade of pink and he could hardly catch his breath. Was she really extending an olive branch?

"Yeah. I'd like that," he murmured then, harnessing every ounce of courage he could find, he reached up and stroked her cheek. "I'd like that very much."

A hesitant smile curved her lips before she cleared her throat.

"I guess I should go get the toppings ready." She turned toward the kitchen. Partway to the doorway, she stopped and turned to face him again. "Thanks, Mark. For all of this." She nodded at the window he was currently working on.

"I'll always keep you safe, Robin. Always."

MAYBE THE WHOLE STALKER/secret admirer thing was a blessing in disguise, Robin thought, changing into a pair of black leggings and a soft white sweater. For the past several weeks, Mark had not only been coming home on time every day after work, he'd been more attentive to her than he'd been in a long while. So much so, she was beginning to remember why she'd fallen in love with him when they were kids. Not that they were old now, barely forty, but they were far from the teens they'd been back then.

Things weren't perfect, she reminded herself, adjusting a narrow black headband in her short blonde hair. Still, they were improving. A lot. She smiled at her reflection in the mirror. As she dabbed perfume on her wrists and behind her ears, she thought about the night before, cuddling on the sofa as they watched a romantic comedy. And about what had happened afterward, something that had been happening a lot more lately. Yeah, not perfect but heading in that direction.

Looking what she hoped was her best, Robin walked back downstairs to check on the baked potatoes. Close enough to done, she removed the roaster pan, turned the oven off, and closed the door. The heat would finish cooking them. She moved the tender, fresh ham carefully to the serving platter, then strained the broth she'd make into gravy for the leftovers they'd enjoy tomorrow.

It wasn't Mark's most favorite meal—she wasn't feeling *that* hopeful yet—but it rated near the top of his list.

They'd been taking the steps they needed to get their marriage back on track and she was going to give a hundred percent, the same as he was doing. The alternative didn't bear thinking about. More than two decades was too long to just turn her back on. There was no question a divorce would break the girls' hearts either.

In truth, it would break hers too.

The doorbell interrupted her thoughts. She opened the door to find their mailman on the porch. He held out the day's post and Robin's stomach clenched when she saw the small box hidden beneath the envelopes.

"Hey, Mrs. Pruitt. I just wanted to thank you for the gift card. The missus and I had a great supper last night."

"You're welcome, Garrett. I thought with the new baby, you could both use a break," she told him, forcing attention away from the package and back to the young man. He'd replaced their former postal worker a couple of years ago and she'd developed a soft spot for him. He was grinning sheepishly, his cheeks flushed from more than just the February air. Robin chuckled. "You took Ariana along, didn't you?"

"Yeah. Sharon wasn't having any part of leaving her with a sitter but we had a nice time anyway."

"I'm glad to hear it." A little more chitchat and she was closing the cold out and heading back to the kitchen.

Sitting down at the counter, she opened a couple of bills, trying to pretend the box wasn't there. But it was and she finally turned her gaze to glare at it. Since the day at the store, her 'admirer' had sent a box of chocolates, a book of poetry and a CD filled with dozens of romantic songs. There'd been nothing for the past couple of weeks though so they'd hoped it was over. That whoever it was had moved on.

Maybe this gift was from Mark, she thought hopefully. Valentine's Day was tomorrow. Maybe he'd sent her something early? Except she knew he wouldn't do anything like this. Not after everything that had happened. Not when he knew it would scare her. And she was definitely scared, her heart pounding in her chest like someone cranked the volume and base up on a hard rock song. Hands shaking, she retrieved a pair of rubber gloves from the towel drawer.

Moments later, Robin stared open mouthed flimsy piece of fabric in her hands like it was a venomous spider or moldy piece of garbage. A sheer red negligee, she was sure the shade was a stark contrast to the pale white her face must be now that the blood had drained out of it. The thought of a stranger sending her something so personal, so—*intimate*—sent chills down her spine, and they weren't the nice kind either. Trembling harder now, she could barely hold the card that had fallen out of the box.

Hey, sexy lady. Perhaps you might consider wearing this some evening when the lights are low. I imagine how lovely you'd look, standing there in front of the French doors, the firelight dancing behind you. Just the thought fans the flames of my desire. Perhaps we should consider getting rid of your husband so I can have you all to myself.

Her first thought was that he'd just described her family room. The family room located at the back of the house. The family room that could only be seen from the backyard—or the woods beyond it.

Her second and more frightening one was—had he just threatened Mark?

Heart in her throat, Robin slid off the stool and, keeping close to the walls, she crept through the house closing the drapes and curtains in each room. Part of her felt stupid, but another part worried, was he out there now? Peering in windows? Watching her?

Knees shaking, she sat down on a stool at the counter, glaring at the box and its contents. Should she call someone? Mark? He'd been getting progressively more stressed with each delivery. She was afraid this one might send him over the edge.

The police? Would they take this seriously? This *gift* that was so vastly different from the rest because it was now clear his intentions weren't innocent. Robin didn't even want to think what he might send next. What he might *do* to both her and her husband.

Chapter 3

Something smelled good, Mark thought, inhaling appreciatively as he walked into the kitchen. He loved pork and wasn't surprised to find that his wife had decided to serve it for supper. The only thing that would have made it better is if she'd been there to greet him, maybe with more kisses like the ones they'd been sharing lately. Like the ones they'd shared the night before...

He felt warmth spread through him as he hung his coat in the closet. Things had improved so much it almost felt like they were newlyweds again. No, he wasn't a young kid anymore, but he was definitely giving his twenty-year-old self a run for the money.

The smile he'd been wearing at the thought of 'later' faded when he saw Robin sitting at the counter. She was staring at something in her hands, the expression on her face one he'd come to recognize. Another package. When she glanced up at him, she looked more afraid than she had with the others and he hurried to her side.

"He knows what our family room looks like," she whispered, leaning into him. "And he threatened you, Mark. He wants to get rid of you."

He wrapped his arms around her, holding her tight as he thumbed through the screen on his phone. He'd added the number for the local police to his contacts list after the flowers had come. He'd truly hoped the day would never come when they'd need it. Unfortunately, it had and as he listened to the ringing on the other end, he glared at the negligee. Oh to find whoever was doing this... He'd like five minutes alone with him. Just five minutes.

"Could you send an officer," he asked when a woman answered. "Someone is stalking my wife and I'm afraid she might be in danger."

And he was. More afraid than he'd ever been before. The thought of someone hurting her filled him with rage—and a desire to deal with this without the aid of the law.

ROBIN PUT THE ROAST back in the broth and covered it with foil in hopes that it would still be moist and tender after they'd filed the complaint. And then she sat back down at the counter as her husband paced from the kitchen to the family room and back. Over and over and over. Pacing. It's what he'd always done when he was worried, at least since she'd met him and that had been a long time ago. It was a habit that had never changed.

Trying to keep the fear at bay, she watched him, this man she'd been married to for more than half her life. In many ways, he hadn't changed at all. Sure, his hair was more silver than black now, years earlier than it should have turned, but he wore it well. He also sported a neatly trimmed beard and mustache. He was still dependable, still a hard worker, still strong, and smart, and funny. Still a sexy, generous lover. And taking care of his family was still his first priority.

How had she forgotten all of those things?

"Mark?" she said softly, reaching out her hand when he neared her again.

He hesitated for a moment, then he took it and tugged gently until she was standing beside him and he was holding her close. Robin sighed at the strength of the arms wrapped around her, at the solid chest she rested her cheek against.

"I won't let him hurt you," he promised again, his breath warm against her hair.

"I know."

The doorbell pealed, making her jump. He laughed softly and kissed her nose before they headed to the front of the house, his arm around her shoulders. He opened the door to see an officer dressed in navy standing on their porch.

"Mr. and Mrs.—" He glanced down at a small notebook, then back up at them. "Pruitt?"

"Yes," Mark said, nodding.

"I'm Officer McCready. You called about a possible stalking situation?"

"Possible? No, there's no question. It *is* a stalking situation," Mark told him, all warmth in his tone gone. She could tell he was annoyed by the doubt in the officer's question and Robin tightened her arm around his waist to try and calm him.

"Then if I could just get your statement..."

"Please, come in," she invited, looking up at Mark. He finally held the screen open to let the man inside.

They led him to the kitchen where they'd laid out everything she'd been sent, including the long dead flowers. McCready pulled a pair of rubber gloves out of his pocket and put them on before touching anything. After reading each card, he wrote something in the notebook, then looked at them.

"How much have you handled all of this?"

"Well, our fingerprints are all over the vase and first card. We were careful with the rest though."

"That's good."

He pulled a package of plastic zip top bags from his other pocket and bagged each one, along with the card that went with it. Then, after asking a few more questions, he advised them to be careful and to call the department if anything else happened. And then he was on his way.

"Did he strike you as not especially worried?" Mark asked later as they sat down to their late supper.

Fortunately, it wasn't ruined but Robin didn't enjoy it as much as she might have before the mail had come. She didn't think he was getting much pleasure from it either.

"I don't know. He didn't laugh at us or try to make us feel stupid." She watched Mark take a slow breath.

"I guess I wanted him to offer round-the-clock protection or something." He laughed a short, mocking laugh. "Like that would ever happen. Their budget isn't that big."

"No, it's not." She reached across the table and stroked the back of the hand he'd laid on the tabletop. "We'll be okay, Mark."

"It's not *we* I'm worried about. It's you."

"Well it's *you* I'm worried about now." The thought of him being hurt... She just couldn't bear it if something happened to him.

Mark helped clean up when they were finished eating, then put an action movie in the DVD player. She curled up next to him but when they spent most of the first half an hour necking, he turned it off and carried her up to bed.

Later, lying with her head on his shoulder, her hand resting against his warm chest, she thought she could stay there forever and be happy.

"We should take a vacation," he murmured, lightly caressing her back.

"Where?"

"Anywhere you like. Name it and I'll take you there."

"Jamaica?"

"Works for me. I'll let my boss know and see if I can get it arranged next week."

"Next week? Wait. Mark? You're serious, aren't you?" she asked, rising up on her elbow to stare at him. In the dim light filtering in from a nearby streetlamp, she could see that he *was* serious.

"Yeah. Of course I am."

"We can't take a vacation just like that."

"Sure we can," he told her, pulling her back down until she was lying against him again. "I've got almost two months' time off coming to me and we might as well use some of it. What do you think? Three or four weeks?"

"Why?"

"Because we haven't taken a vacation in too long."

"Mark..." He sighed as she pressed him for the truth, though she was fully aware of the reason.

"Because I want to get you somewhere safe," he admitted, pressing his lips against her hair.

"But—"

"But what?"

"What if he gets in our house while we're away? Right now, the longest the house is empty is when you're working and I'm at the store. That doesn't bother me too much because our neighbors are kind of nosy but if we were gone for weeks—" She shivered at the thought of someone going through their things. Mark pulled her closer.

"All right. We'll stay home then. I am going to get a security system installed though. Door alarms. Window alarms. Motion sensors in the yard. The works."

"That, I could go for," she said, sighing. He really did take the best care of her.

Chapter 4

Just because Robin didn't want to leave the house didn't mean they couldn't have a 'stay-cation,' Mark decided. After explaining the situation to his boss, he punched out with two and a half weeks off—and the promise of more time if he needed it.

On the way home, he stopped at one of the local combination grocery/department stores. Not only was it Valentine's Day, it was also mid-February in Michigan. Gone were parkas, electric blankets, and sidewalk salt. Sixteen degrees outside and their shelves and clothing racks were stocked with all manner of spring and summer items.

Like a man on a mission, he sped through the store grabbing one item after another. He knew what he wanted, and where to find it, so he was only half an hour late pulling into the garage. Entering the house with three bulging shopping bags, he grinned at Robin.

"What's all that?" she asked, smiling back at him from where she stood at the counter. She was shredding the leftover meat as the pot of broth simmered on the stove. On another burner, sliced potatoes were frying on low. Another one of his favorite meals. Hot pork sandwiches and crispy hash browns smothered in rich, thick gravy.

"Surprises," he said, crossing the room to stand beside her.

He leaned down to kiss her, slowly, in a sort of preview of coming attractions. He almost forgot his plan when she melted against him with a soft moan.

"What kind of surprises?" she asked, long moments later, her voice low and breathless. He took a calming breath. And then he took another one, his gaze moving between her and the counter. Robin laughed softly, reading his mind.

"Well, for one thing, our new—attire," he finally told her, working hard to get his passion under control. This was supposed to be fun and light. There would be plenty of time for honeymoon activities later. "Come upstairs when you're finished. I'm going to go change now."

After another kiss that had his blood rushing again, he hurried up to their room, hiding out in the bathroom until he heard her come in.

"Mark? Where are the clothes?"

"On the bed," he told her, cracking the door open just a little, watching her like a peeping Tom.

"No. There are only a pile of leis on the bed."

"Look under them."

He heard her giggle, then walked out wearing nothing but a pair of orange and yellow swimming trunks—and two blue leis that clashed like the girls chose the colors. When they were two. Holding up the tiny scraps of fabric that comprised a yellow bikini, Robin turned red.

"Yours has about a hundred times more fabric than mine," she said, but raised a hand to the top button on her blouse.

Mark felt his skin start to prickle as she unfastened it, taking her time as she moved to the next one. And the one after that. And the one after that. Her eyes never left his and he felt like a teenager getting his first look at a girlie magazine. Except his wife was better than any model in any magazine he'd ever seen. He could tell from her barely there smile that she knew what she was doing to him and he had to clear his throat a couple of times before he could speak.

"Well, it was this or a Speedo and, well, no. Just no." Only one of them looked good in a skimpy bathing suit and it wasn't him.

"So... We're aiming for a romantic supper?" She'd reached the last button now and Mark swallowed hard.

"Actually, more like a romantic two and a half weeks." She raised her brows as she dropped the blouse on the bed. "Just because we're staying home doesn't mean we can't have a vacation. I don't have to be back until March sixth and I decided since we'll be all alone here, we might as well turn the house into our own personal Eden."

"Eden?"

"Yeah. I'll be Adam and you'll be Eve. Unfortunately, I couldn't find any fig leaves so we'll have to settle for these." He fingered the leis around his neck as he watched his wife slowly shed the rest of her clothes.

"So we actually have," he watched her count on her fingers, "almost three weeks?"

"Yes." He hoped he didn't look as desperate as he felt as he ogled his wife.

"So what's on the agenda for tomorrow?" she asked after she'd shimmied into the bikini. Mark picked up the pink leis and slipped them over her head.

"Well, tomorrow is the wrench in the works. The security company is coming to install the alarms so we'll have to wear normal clothes until they leave. But then, it's right back to this."

He started reaching into the bags, pulling out a few more trunks for him and half a dozen more suits for her. Beach towels, cheesy cups shaped like pineapples and coconuts, and several summery scented candles followed everything else onto the dresser.

"So we're going to pretend we're at the beach for the next few weeks?"

"Yep. We'll probably want to keep the curtains closed."

"So the neighbors don't have us locked up for walking around half naked in the middle of winter?"

"Something like that," he said, stepping closer to her. He reached up to stroke her cheek. "Consider this our second honeymoon."

"Sounds like it might be better than our first," she whispered as he leaned down so his lips were a breath away from hers.

"Oh it will be. Trust me," he whispered back, kissing her until she trembled in his arms. "Will supper wait?"

"Supper?"

LATER, SITTING IN FRONT of the fireplace on the beach towels, they were finally digging in to their very late supper. For ambiance, Mark turned the lights off, lit a few candles, and streamed a video with waves washing up on shore to the flat screen. It wasn't a tropical beach but close enough for horseshoes.

"Do you remember how we used to walk everywhere when it was nice outside?" Robin asked, spearing a piece of meat and popping it in her mouth.

"Yeah, it was the only way your folks would let us go on dates for longer than two hours."

Technically, her parents hadn't cared how much time they spent together—as long as it was at their house when one of them was home, or on foot around town. They just couldn't be alone in an enclosed space without a chaperone. Mom and Dad Burkhart had made it clear they weren't taking a chance on becoming grandparents before graduation.

Back then, the two of them used to joke about feeling like they were living in the eighteen hundreds but they didn't mind the rules. Not as long as they could be together.

So Mark often left his old clunker at home and they'd covered miles and miles strolling up one street and down another. Sometimes, they'd hold hands across a picnic table in one of the parks, staring at each other like a couple of goofy celebrities in a sappy romance movie.

"You made me feel—I don't know. Like I was the most special girl in the world." She couldn't quite meet his gaze as she said the words, but peered up at him through her lashes after they were out.

"That's because you were. You still *are*." She saw a cloud of sadness in his eyes. "I'm sorry I ever made you feel like you weren't. Robin, you are and always will be the most special girl in the world to me. Even when we're ninety-nine, hobbling around with canes, gumming the soft foods they're feeding us at the nursing home, and wearing hearing aids with the volume turned off so everyone has to yell when they talk to us." They both laughed at the image his description brought to mind.

"You never made me feel like I wasn't," she said, reaching out to stroke his cheek. If they took anymore of their meals in the family room, she decided, they were sharing a single towel. Even though they were only separated by their plates, they were still too far apart. "I think we just got so busy with the girls, and ball games, and dance recitals, we kind of got lost in the shuffle."

"Whatever it was, I promise it won't happen again. Much as I love the girls, I love you more." He leaned forward to kiss her softly. "You are the most important thing in the world, Robin. I was so afraid of losing you—" Eyes brighter than they'd been a moment ago, she watched him blink the tears away. "I didn't know if we'd survive when they moved out."

"I didn't think we would either." She took a slow, shaky breath, then smiled at this man she'd loved most of her life. "Much as I hate all of this stalking stuff, in a way I'm glad it happened. I know it sounds weird but... I don't know how to explain it without sounding like a lunatic."

"I know what you mean. I really hope the police catch whoever is sending you that stuff, sweetheart. Soon. Because part of me wants to beat him to a pulp for scaring you, but another part wants to thank him too."

"Maybe you could beat him up first?" She suggested, then laughed, even as she wiped at a tear rolling down her cheek. "As long as we don't lose each other again. Ever. I've missed you so much, Mark."

Chapter 5

"**Y**ou are such a cheater!" Robin accused, laughing as she peeled the sock off her right foot. "That's not a real word!"

On the way home from the grocery store, Mark suggested a game of cutthroat strip Scrabble. So far, she'd mostly drawn a variety of consonants and now she was down to her underwear and one sock. All he'd lost was a single shoe and his sweater.

"It certainly *is* a word," he said smugly, thumbing through the dictionary until he found *bezoar.* When he held it out to her, Robin read the definition and shuddered. He chuckled when she wrinkled her nose at him.

"Why do you even know that word? A mass in a goat's stomach?" she asked, shaking her head.

"I'm just a fount of strange and useless information. It comes in handy sometimes. Like now. Just because you've lost more clothes than I have... Well, I'm totally okay with that."

When she had to trade another tile a while later, he waggled his brows and wanted to know what she was taking off this time. He laughed when, without hesitation, she removed her last sock.

"Good thing it's warm in here because after I make this word, you might get a little chilly. Of course, if you want to scoot over here, I'll keep you warm."

"*Only* warm?" she teased.

"Really, *really* warm," he promised, turning his attention to the tiles.

Emptying his rack, he spelled out *physical.* Kind of appropriate, she thought, given that they'd be getting very physical when the game was over.

He leaned across the coffee table and kissed her slowly, not stopping until he heard her breath hitch. She almost suggested ending the game but it was too much fun. Mark was getting a kick out of it and, if she had to be honest, the game was pretty darned sexy. So she was determined to wait until one of them lost. Right now, it was looking like the loser would be her. The quicker she lost though, the quicker they'd both win.

Much to her surprise though, she got him down to his socks before he finally won. Gazing into her eyes, he got up, rounded the table, and pulled her into his arms and she'd never been so happy to lose anything in her life.

ROBIN WASN'T SURE WHAT to think of this new version of her husband. But he wasn't a new version at all. It was actually the return of the normal, fun loving man who'd gotten a little lost under the demands and responsibilities of taking care of his family. She was glad he was back, especially since his mission in life—at the moment—seemed to be turning the clock back twenty years.

When he'd said a second honeymoon, he hadn't been exaggerating. She'd been right about it being better than the first though. When they'd gone to Hawaii following their wedding, they'd spent much of the time visiting popular tourist attractions. This time, the vast majority of their time was spent together, cuddling, talking, playing silly games like the strip Scrabble and hide-n-seek. And making love. She'd begun to feel like a new bride during their first exciting days together.

The only cloud on their otherwise idyllic vacation was the arrival of a used, well-read copy of a best-selling BDSM novel. Neither one of them had ever read it but thanks to the publicity surrounding its release, knew what it was about.

What scared her most though was within minutes of the delivery, she got a phone call. Already shaken by the book, she didn't even think to see if she recognized the number. When she answered, there was only music. A popular song with lyrics about a stalker keeping tabs on everything his target was doing, even breathing. More than ever, she feared the plans he might have for her.

Mark phoned the police immediately.

A new guy came this time, Officer Duncan. They both felt better when he seemed concerned, taking the *gifts* the same way she and Mark did, as threats. When he left, they were confident the investigation would be ramped up and whoever was sending the things would be found. Soon.

By the next morning, they'd pretended enough so they were able to recapture the carefree atmosphere, mostly, and they started the day off with a big breakfast.

Early into the vacation, Mark surprised her. Being a stay-at-home mom since the girls' birth, she'd taken care of everything inside the house but he'd not only been doing some cleaning, he'd taken over some of the cooking as well. Especially breakfasts. And she'd thought his kitchen skills ended at pouring a cup of coffee.

But there he was, standing at the stove wearing a pair of those awful bathing trunks—and a full length red and white checkered apron, frying bacon and hash browns. She threatened to snap a picture and post it on Facebook for the girls to see.

"If you want all their friends drooling over me, go ahead," he dared her, grinning when she did exactly that.

"Well, that was quick," she said, laughing when a comment from their youngest twin popped up almost immediately.

"What?"

"Alexis saw it already." Mark snickered.

"What did she say?"

"Mom! Really???" It was quickly followed by, "What's Dad doing home on a Friday morning? I didn't know he could cook."

"And not just in the kitchen," he reminded her, trying to leer but not quite pulling it off.

They both laughed and Robin was sorry their perfect vacation was nearly over. Two more days and life would be back to normal. Oh how she wished he could retire now but he wouldn't have his thirty years in for another decade. Even though they had a nice savings account and had invested wisely, they would still need his pension. And that meant he had to keep showing up for work.

"Hey, why so quiet?" Mark asked, setting a plate of bacon on the counter in front of her.

"Just wishing Monday wasn't so close. I kind of like having you home."

"Kind of?" he teased. Robin jumped up and threw her arms around his neck.

"I *love* having you home," she told him, then whispered, "I'm going to miss you."

"We'll plan more holidays like this," he promised holding her close, and she hoped he meant it.

THREE DAYS. IT HAD only been three days and Robin still wasn't used to being alone in the house again. They still spent every second together they could after work but during the daytime hours, she missed Mark like crazy. He must have missed her too because for the first time ever, he was texting her. And not just the, 'do you need me to pick up anything on my way home' kind of text either.

I wanted you to know that I'm thinking about you—and counting the hours until I get home.

Hey, sexy lady, how about putting on that little black dress that's hanging in our closet? We'll go to the English Inn and then find a movie we want to see. Or we could just go home and spend some quality time together.

Of course, she opted for the quality time. She always would. But there was still a third of her day to get through until he got home again and she was bored out of her mind.

One morning, the girls sent her a message asking if she had time for a video chat. Robin snorted. She had all the time in the world and jumped on the invitation like a drowning man on a life preserver.

"Wow, you're looking great, Mom," Haley said as soon as her face appeared on the screen.

"Hey, did you get your hair cut?" Alexis demanded, peeking around her sister's head to peer at her mother. "Because you look—hmm. I don't want to say beautiful because you always look beautiful. I just can't quite put my finger on it."

"Happy," Haley murmured, nodding her blonde head slowly. "She looks happy."

"That's it! What are you doing that's making you look so happy, Mom?"

"I don't know," Robin hedged, thinking her acting skills sucked as much now as they had in her tenth grade drama class. "I didn't know I looked *un*happy."

"Come on. You've been looking like someone killed your best dog for months. And you know us. We're not going to stop until you fess up." She sighed because Haley was right. They wouldn't.

"All right. Fine. Your father and I—"

"No! They're getting a divorce. I knew it," Alexis wailed, smacking her sister on the arm. Haley's face fell too.

"Your father and I are *not* getting a divorce," she assured them quickly. "We *were* having some problems but, well, we kind of had a second honeymoon and everything is fine now."

"A second honeymoon?" Alexis leaned down and put her head so close to Haley's that Haley had to move so only half her face was visible on the screen. "Where did you go? And why didn't you tell us?"

"We didn't go anywhere. Just stayed here and got to know each other again."

"That sounds boring."

"Well it wasn't. Trust me, it was anything *but* boring." Robin felt her cheeks color when she realized how they might interpret that.

"And I think we can change the subject now." She disappeared from the screen but not before Robin saw her youngest—by two and a half minutes—turn beet red too.

"We talked a lot," she told them, changing the subject. No, that wasn't all they'd done, but they had spent a lot of time discussing the past and how they never wanted to take each other for granted again.

"So Dad finally took a vacation?" Haley asked after a few moments of uncomfortable silence.

"Yeah. Two and a half weeks."

"Wow. That's a long time for Mr. Workaholic."

"I know. But he's going to start taking more time off here and there. And I hope the next time is soon."

"Miss him that much?"

"Yes. But I've also realized how boring my life has become." As the words left her lips, she was struck again at just how dull it was. Yes, she did miss Mark, but she'd also begun to depend on him, to entertain her, to give her life a purpose she hadn't felt since the girls left for college.

"You're not having a mid-life crisis, are you?" The worry was back in Haley's voice. Like maybe she might get bored with her marriage.

"Not really. But now that you two are on your own, there isn't much for me to do. Cleaning doesn't take long, neither does laundry for two. And while I love to read, there's more to life than sweeping and books."

"What about writing them instead? You used to tell Alexis and me the best stories. Maybe you could write books for kids. Or any other kind you want. I know the community college has courses. You could take one or two and see if it's something you'd like to do. Or you could look into photography so you can take the family portraits when the grandkids start arriving. You can do anything you want, Mom."

"*Grandkids!* Is there something I need to know about?" she demanded, feeling faint at the thought. She was too young to be a grandma!

"No. But it's going to happen someday," Haley said, chuckling. "Just looking ahead to save some money."

Chapter 6

"So... I was thinking about taking a couple of classes."

They were enjoying a candlelight supper and Robin was telling him about her conversation with the girls. He wasn't surprised they'd noticed something amiss though he thought he and Robin had hidden it well over the holidays. Apparently not. At least everyone was happy now, especially his wife.

"I did a little research afterward and I don't think I'd want to write stories for small children. But there were a few I made up for Haley and Alexis that I could easily turn into young adult fantasies." She tilted her head, her nose scrunched a little. "Do you think it's a totally stupid idea?"

"I don't think it's stupid at all. I know I've never owned up to this but sometimes, I'd stand outside their bedroom door and listen while you spun your tales. They were pretty interesting, Robin," he admitted sheepishly. "So if it's something you want to do, I say go for it. It'll be fun to have all three of my girls in college." He hated to add a caveat but had to say, "As long as you don't use the parking garage."

"Yeah, I thought about that too. But maybe by the time the spring term starts, they'll have caught the guy."

"I don't like the idea of you being alone in a parking garage under any circumstances so just promise me you'll park on the street. Please?"

"I promise."

Now he wished he'd insisted Robin sign up for the same self-defense courses they'd signed the girls up for when they'd turned thirteen. Each year, they'd participated in a refresher course because he didn't want to send them out into the world unprepared. He decided he'd talk to the instructor about getting his wife on the schedule as soon as possible. This whole stalker thing had shaken him to the core and he needed to make sure they did everything in their power to keep her safe.

After they cleaned up the supper mess, they cuddled on the sofa with the laptop while Robin showed him one thing after another. She'd need a website where she could blog—about what, she wasn't sure yet—and start to build a social media platform, something he was familiar with given his position as a senior partner in a web designing business. He was looking forward to working with his wife, helping to make her latent dreams of becoming an author come true.

"MR. PRUITT? WE NEED to talk." Officer Duncan stood on their porch again, one of the girls' good friends, Martin Abrams, standing beside him.

They both looked ill at ease as Mark opened the door to let them in. He led them to the family room where Robin sat at the desk, typing everything she could remember of the stories she'd made up into a file on the laptop, something she'd been doing each day since their talk a few days ago.

"Honey?" he said, walking to her side and putting a hand on her shoulder. She glanced up at him, then at the men standing behind him.

"Hey, Martin," she said with a smile before glancing at Mark, brows drawn together in confusion. He just shrugged as she got to her feet.

"Hey, Mrs. Pruitt." Yeah, the kid looked really uncomfortable, glancing briefly at her, then staring at his feet. Officer Duncan cleared his throat.

"The fine piece of literature you received had a stamp on the inside cover. It was for the bookstore where it was purchased so I paid the owner a visit. She remembered the transaction because Mr. Abrams is a regular customer but until then, he'd only been interested in stories about wizards and space aliens. She said he acted strange that day, wouldn't meet her eyes, and was blushing to the roots of his hair."

Kind of like now, Robin thought, working hard to keep a straight face. Mark, on the other hand, wasn't working to control his facial expression at all. He was mad. Maybe a little more than mad. Furious.

"It was *you*, Martin? *You're* the guy who's in love with *my wife?*" he demanded, taking a step toward the boy, his stance menacing. Robin reached out for his hand to hold him back but before she could say a word, Martin's head snapped up and he looked like he'd just been told to scrape the bottom of a trash can and have it for supper.

"*In love with—*" He shook his head violently. "With *Mrs. Pruitt?* Eww! No! That's gross. She's old enough to be my *mother!*"

Robin bit her bottom lip hard in an effort to hold back the laughter that was begging to escape. For a moment, she wondered if she should feel a little insulted but decided it was too funny to be offended over.

"Then why in the world did you send her all that stuff? The nightgown? *The book?* Do you know you scared her—scared both of us half to death?"

"I didn't mean to!" He looked at them now, thoroughly chastised. "I swear I didn't."

"Here's where the problem comes in, Mr. Pruitt. It's why I brought Mr. Abrams here before deciding whether to arrest him or not." All color left Martin's face at that and Robin really wanted to give him a hug, to tell him it was all right. A psychologist would probably have a field day with her over that reaction but darn it, she felt sorry for the kid.

"What problem?" Mark asked, glaring at Martin.

"Well, he says your daughters put him up to it."

"That's a lie! They would never ask anyone to stalk Robin!"

"Stalk her? No, no, no! They wanted me to send stuff to make you jealous, Mr. Pruitt. They were afraid you were going to get a divorce and thought if you saw that some guy was sending stuff to your wife, you'd …

well, I'm not sure what they thought you'd do but they thought it would help."

Mark shot her a look that was as shocked as hers must have been. They'd been worried enough they'd shared their fears with Martin? She couldn't think about that right now though because the boy in question kept talking, trying to explain that his only crime was doing a favor for friends. Robin had to keep biting her lip but she wasn't the only one who found his story hilarious. The corners of Officer Duncan's lips kept twitching and it looked as though his jaws were clamped together tight.

It seemed the girls had given him fifty dollars—and instructions to send her gifts over a period of weeks.

"Those flowers cost almost half of what they gave me and that was just for the first week. I really didn't know what to do after that because, well, I haven't had all that much experience with girls and I didn't think Mr. Pruitt would get jealous over trading cards or stuff *I'm* interested in."

And so he'd turned to a few of his buddies. He did not, he assured them, name names, just asked for ideas of what he could do to make a guy jealous enough to pay more attention to his girl. The one they all considered to be the most experienced came up with and wrote all the notes. Then they tossed out ideas for inexpensive gifts, stuff he could pick up at resale shops. Ideas for things that would make *them* jealous.

"I guess I should have told them it was for an old couple and I needed ideas that weren't sexy or romantic."

Mark finally seemed to find the humor in the situation and his eyes met hers. She knew he was thinking the same thing he was. *Old couples* were totally into sexy, romantic things. Just not from strangers. When Martin finally asked, "You're not gonna tell my mom, are you," her husband burst out laughing. Soon, she and the officer joined him. Martin just looked at them as though they'd lost their minds.

Chapter 7

"**G**ood grief, Martin!" Less than two hours later, Haley was on her feet, hands on her hips, delivering a lecture that had her friend cringing. "We told you to make him jealous, not *terrorize* them! No wonder they thought Mom had a stalker! What in the world were you thinking, sending her a sexy nightgown and *that book*? And that phone call? I can't believe you played that creepy song! What were you thinking!"

Martin was sitting on the edge of the sofa, hands clasped between his knees, head hung low.

"I don't know."

"We told you to send flowers and candy and stuff like that."

"Well after the flowers and candy, you should have told me what you meant by the other stuff."

"Okay, that's enough," Robin finally said, trying to hide another smile. Now that she knew she'd never had a stalker, that it was just a young man trying to do a favor for her daughters, her attitude about the situation had done an about face. Now she felt the need to defend the boy. "He didn't exactly *mean* to terrorize us. And Martin is right. What else was he supposed to send?"

"Mom," Alexis said with a long-suffering sigh. "He scared you and dad out of twenty years of your life."

"Only a year," Mark said, tongue-in-cheek, rolling his eyes at their drama queens. "Maybe two, but nowhere near twenty. So give the guy a break, okay."

"Yeah, give me a break. I was doing you a favor. Remember? And it worked, didn't it?"

"Yeah, it did," her husband agreed, a tender smile on his face when he looked at his wife. "I'm sorry things got to the place where you felt you had to resort to something like this, but it worked very well. So cut the guy a break. Tell Martin thank you—and by the way, *thank you*, Martin—and let him go home already."

"*You're* welcome." Robin nearly laughed at the look the boy flashed her husband, like it was the two of them against the world.

"Tell him thank you," she echoed, fixing each girl with a stern stare. After a few moments, they grinned and hugged their friend, who then made tracks for the front door. There, he glanced over his shoulder at her.

"I really am sorry I scared you, Mrs. Pruitt. I didn't mean to."

"I know. And it's okay. Just—don't send me anymore gifts, okay?" she asked, her tone teasing. Martin grinned, ducked his head, and made his escape, something he'd been dying to do since he and the officer arrived nearly two and a half hours ago.

"It's a good thing it's Friday," Haley said, flopping down on the sofa and looking from her to Mark and back again. "I am sorry, Mom. I guess we should have asked Lucy or Brenda. A *girl* would never have sent you those things. And a used negligee? Good grief! Only Martin would look for something like that at a secondhand store! I hope you washed your hands after you touched it."

"You gave the poor kid fifty dollars," Mark said with a chuckle. "And he had to pay postage for everything too. I'm guessing if you ask, he probably spent some of his own money too."

"If he did, he bought *that book* with it." Alexis shuddered at the thought. "And he sent it to *Mom*. That's just wrong."

"Since you're already here, are you two going to spend the weekend?" Robin asked, changing the subject abruptly.

"Just tonight," Haley said. "Ms. Queen of the Campus has a date tomorrow night so we'll have to leave in time for her to get ready. Got any spare spackle lying around, Dad? She wants to make an impression on this one."

"Oh ha-ha," Alexis said, jabbing her in the side with her elbow.

Ah. Life was back to normal, Robin thought, announcing that she was going to order a couple of pizzas. Mark wrapped an arm around her, kissing her soundly and whispering in her ear. She blushed to the roots of her hair but smiled as she went in search of her phone. Yeah, Martin's efforts might have been a little misguided but thanks to him, her marriage was better than it had ever been.

ROBIN WAS BEGINNING to stir, cuddling against Mark, her head on his shoulder. The girls weren't making much of an effort to be quiet, thumping and bumping around in the room they were sharing again. Haley had been a little dismayed to find she'd been moved back in with her sister but they wouldn't be spending a lot of time at home between now and the time they graduated. After that, they'd be getting their own apartments so there was no reason to wait to turn the third bedroom into an office for their mother. After all, it had been their idea for her to pursue a writing career.

"I love having them home," Robin mumbled, "but I'm not used to how noisy they are anymore."

"I know. They woke me up about half an hour ago."

"Think we should drag ourselves out of bed and get some breakfast around?" she asked, moving her hand so it was splayed across his chest. Normally, now anyway, they'd spend a little quality time in bed before getting up but unlike most kids their age, the girls never had been much into sleeping in.

"Not before I get some coffee. Want a cup?"

"Yes, please."

He hugged her close, then kissed her nose before climbing out of bed and padding to the door.

"Mark!" Robin exclaimed, looking pointedly at his obvious state of undress. She watched her handsome husband grin as he dropped his hand from the doorknob.

"Sorry. I guess I've gotten so used to not needing clothes on every second of every day, I forgot."

"And *that's* more information that I needed to know," Haley's voice sounded from the hallway. "How old are you two?"

"Old enough," Mark shot back, taking the robe Robin retrieved for him before drawing her into his arms and whispering, "you look cute when you blush."

"Next thing I know, you'll be telling me you're joining a nudist camp."

"Yeah, I doubt it," he assured her quickly. "For one thing, there's a big difference between making a quick trip to the kitchen for a cup of coffee and parading around in front of a bunch of naked people. And for another, I'm the only man who gets to ogle your mother."

"Oh please. I'm too young for this conversation. And don't tell Alexis. If she finds out your running around the house like that, it'll be all over town before the day is over."

"It will, too," Robin said with a sigh. Mark nodded. It wasn't that daughter number two meant to be a gossip, it was just—well, she was.

"Tell Alexis what?" Alexis asked from what sounded like her bedroom doorway." Robin leaned her forehead against his chin and started to giggle.

"Nothing," Haley said, slamming the door of the bathroom across the hall.

"What aren't you telling me?" Alexis demanded a moment later, rapping on their door. "I don't like secrets when I don't know what they are."

"I'm making Boeuf Bourguignon for your father after you two head back."

"Boeuf Bourguignon? Why would you keep that a secret?"

'No reason," Robin told her, laughing softly when she walked away muttering about crazy parents and a loony sister.

"Really?" he asked, pulling her closer. "You're really going to make it for supper?"

"Yes, I am. And an apple pie too."

It had been ages since she'd made it for him. That particular meal involved lots of slicing and dicing and it took forever, but she'd always made it for him for their special days. Until the last couple of years.

"Is there a special occasion I've forgotten about?" he whispered, kissing her temple, prepared to run out and buy a card and candy if need be.

"Every day is special with you," she whispered back, settling against him in a way that told him the coffee could wait.

Keep reading for a FREE BOOK offer, and a sneak peek from The Daddy Pact, another *FREE* book from Kristy! Get your copy by clicking on the link below:
http://kristykjames.net/books/the-daddy-pact/

FREE BOOK!

Click here http://kristykjames.net/newsletter/to subscribe to my newsletter – and to get your FREE digital copy of Hard Goodbyes and New Beginnings – the prequel for my new Weko Harbor series!

Friends you make as a kid are friends for life in Weko Harbor.
This novella is an introduction to Kristy K. James' new series. In it, you'll
get to meet members of a now grown youth group as they deal with the
death of a beloved mentor – and the return of a friend who has lost his
way.

Sneak Peek: The Daddy Pact

Sitting at his cluttered desk filling out paperwork, Ed Winslow looked more like an office executive than an officer of the law. In his navy suit and nearly matching tie, no one would guess he lived life on the edge, putting himself in danger every day to solve crimes in Michigan's Capitol city.

Chalk another one up for the Lansing Police Department. For Winslow anyway. Working on the case for three and a half months, he'd made the long-awaited call yesterday. It was over, the trial to come a mere formality. Bruce Mulholland, for no apparent reason, had turned himself in, making a full confession. Yes, they had their man, and a guaranteed conviction. Still, he couldn't help but wish-

No matter what he wished, there was nothing to be done now. Nothing to change what had happened. Or what was to come. He'd never liked working on this case. Not from the moment he'd been assigned to it.

The gold pen he held, moving across the page in front of him, stopped. Alerted by a slight sound or movement, or perhaps a sixth sense honed through twenty-odd years of police work, he knew he was being watched. Whatever the reason, he looked up, unable to hide his dismay when he saw her in the doorway.

Running a hand through his short-cropped brown hair, beginning to show signs of gray – and receding more each day, he rose to his feet to greet her. This was the last thing he wanted to deal with now, but he should have known she'd come.

"Mrs. Bentley. This is a surprise." Though his smile welcomed her, he studied her, his thick brows drawn together in thought. "I'm afraid we weren't expecting you today."

"Can I see him?" Jess Bentley asked, voice flat, her green eyes dull, almost vacant. Winslow swore she looked right through him.

"You said you couldn't identify him, even if we did need your help."

"I can't."

"Can't what? Identify him? I know. Look, why don't you have a seat. I'll get you a cup of coffee and we'll talk." He indicated a pair of worn leather chairs in front of his desk.

"I want to see him," she repeated, ignoring his attempt at social pleasantries.

Winslow studied her like a germ under a microscope. The last time he'd seen her, at the funeral, she'd been a typical, run-of-the mill widow, dressed in black, hauntingly beautiful. Today, well, today there was little resemblance to the woman he remembered.

The gray sweat suit she wore was several sizes too large for her slender frame. Wrinkled, it looked as if she'd had it on for several days, probably the same length of time since her hair had seen a brush. The dirty brown locks tumbled down her back in a tangled mess, and dark circles beneath wide-eyes, matched thick sooty lashes, contrasting dramatically with the pallor of her skin.

He also sensed a tenseness emanating from her. From the rigid way she held herself as she stood in the doorway, to the desperate way she clutched a floral tapestry handbag to her chest, holding it so tight her knuckles were white. Something was very wrong here.

"I don't think that's a good idea, ma'am."

"Maybe not, but I still want to."

"Why?"

"Do I need a reason?"

"I think so."

Jess Bentley shifted her gaze away from him and let it drift around the room seeing, but not taking in the wanted posters and bulletin board on the wall. The huge window overlooking the busy street below might not have been there, nor the glass wall separating this office from the desks on the other side. What she did notice, and Winslow knew the exact moment she did, was the portrait of his former family. He sensed, more than saw, her resentment at its presence. Finally, she looked at him again.

"Nice family."

"Thank you." He rounded the corner of the desk, leaning against its edge, casually crossing his arms as he continued to watch her, waiting patiently for her answer.

"He killed Frank."

"I'm aware of that."

"Isn't that reason enough?"

"Is that the only one?"

"No, it's not." For the first time since her arrival, her voice betrayed the anger she felt. "I want to see the man who murdered my husband. I want him to see that, because of him, I'm alone now."

"It was an accident," Winslow murmured, as though to himself.

"What?"

"It was an accident," he repeated, louder this time. "Mulholland only intended to rob your husband. The shooting wasn't intentional."

"Is that supposed to make everything all right?" Mrs. Bentley asked.

"No, of course not. What I'm saying is if the purpose of this visit is to make him feel guilty then it's a waste of time. You can rest assured, he feels guilty."

"Good. Then maybe I can make him feel worse, hmm?" she asked on a sob.

"Mrs. Bentley," Winslow sighed, "do you realize if he hadn't turned himself in, we'd never have caught him? Not on the evidence we had. He could have gotten away with it, and no one would have been the wiser."

"So give him a medal. I still want to see him, face to face."

Sighing deeply, Winslow shrugged and crossed the room, coming to a stop before a filing cabinet next to where she stood.

He pulled an enormous ring of keys from his jacket pocket, searched for the right one, and unlocked the top drawer. He saw her wince at the ear-piercing squeal as he slid it open.

"Guess I'd better call maintenance," he said by way of apology, holding out his hand. "Just let me lock your bag in here, and I'll take you down."

"No."

"No?"

"I'd rather keep it with me," she stammered, holding it even closer.

"I'm sorry, but I can't allow you in the visiting area unless you leave it here," he explained, his tone gentle.

"It's not like I'd try to help him escape or anything."

"I never thought you would. But that's the rule."

"Can't you bend them? Just this once?" Her eyes pleaded with him to make an exception.

"No, ma'am."

She sagged against the door casing, tears streaming down her face. Winslow put a comforting hand on her shoulder. "Mrs. Bentley, I can't even begin to imagine the pain, the anger, you must be feeling. But I can understand how you might feel the need to take the law into your own hands. And I can't let you do that."

"I knew you knew," she whispered, wiping a hand across her cheeks.

"I don't know anything. I do have my suspicions though. And if I don't go with my gut on this, you'll be the one to suffer."

"Can't that be my choice?"

"No. Mulholland and a witness both said the gun went off when your husband thought you were in danger. Your safety, your life, meant more to him than his own. I won't let you do something that will put you at risk."

"My life?" she asked, laughing harshly. "My life ended when Frank's heart stopped beating. And all that's left is this, this pain and this aloneness." Slender fingers covered her lips as she began to weep.

"Mrs. Bentley." Winslow felt a lump form in his throat as he put an arm around her shoulders. Few cases had ever touched him in this way, and he really wished this one hadn't. He didn't like feeling this helpless. Not one bit. "Ma'am, what you want to do won't take those feelings away. Only time will help."

'No." She shook her head at his lame attempt to comfort her.

"I know it doesn't seem that way now, but it will," he promised. "You just need someone to help you through this. Someone you trust." But who? If he remembered correctly, she had no family and her husband's only relative blamed her for his death.

Winslow couldn't deal with this. It was easier if he could remain detached from a victim's pain. From the perpetrator's pain. He shouldn't be wishing he could find a way to help. But there had to be something. Wait, there had been a friend. Manning? No, that wasn't right. It was Lanning. Emmerald Lanning.

"Did you drive yourself here, Mrs. Bentley?"

"I took a cab." Most likely she hadn't planned on returning to her apartment, he guessed.

"Then I'll take you home. Let me just go and clear it with my boss. It'll only take a minute." He hesitated for a moment before asking, "Which door did you come in?"

"I waited at the side of the building until someone came out."

He'd known it had to be something like that, because she for sure hadn't come in through the front door. Not with security being as tight as it was. Obviously, it left a little to be desired if she'd gotten in another way.

"Wait here. We'll leave that same way."

Winslow spun around, hurrying down the hall to his captain's office, rapping on the glass with more force than necessary and, when the command came to enter, rushing inside and briefly explaining the situation.

"Her home and work numbers should be in the file. Tell Lanning to get to Mrs. Bentley's A.S.A.P."

For the first time in as long as he could remember, Winslow wasn't cussing as he caught almost every stop light on their slow trip across town. He didn't even mind the miles of lunch hour traffic today. The longer the drive, the better the odds were that Mrs. Lanning would be waiting when they arrived.

And that would be a good thing because Mrs. Bentley hadn't uttered a word since climbing into his inconspicuous black sedan. It worried him. If he had to make a guess, he would say that she was in shock. At this moment, he figured, she had probably counted on being in a jail cell, or dead, not riding beside him headed back to her empty apartment. Not with the man she hated alive and well.

He was disappointed to note the absence of the tall black woman waiting on the landing outside her door. Now he didn't know what to do but offer, as they ascended the stairs to her apartment, to stay with her a while.

"No," she said.

"Are you sure?" It wouldn't be any trouble," he assured her. Just until the friend got there.

"I'm sure. I'd really rather be alone."

Stopping at her door, she turned to look over the railing. There it was. The spot where it happened. He knew because there was a faint stain marring the otherwise light-colored pavement. A bloodstain that hadn't washed away after all this time. Her husband's blood. The landlord had obviously tried to clean it up after the investigation, but faint traces still remained.

"I hate leaving you like this," Winslow muttered, rubbing his chin and staring at her hard.

"I'll be fine," she murmured, turning to put her key in the lock. Suddenly she looked back at the detective and asked, "Could you do something for me?"

"Name it."

"Tell him for me that Frank was a good man. Tell him we were happy."

"I can do that," he promised, turning away, hoping she hadn't noticed the lie he'd just told her. "Could you do something for me?"

"What?"

"Take care of yourself."

She didn't answer, only closed the door between them as Winslow walked away, hoping the friend would come soon.

DANIEL MULHOLLAND STOOD at the patio door staring vacantly at the rolling hills behind his home. He didn't feel pride of ownership like he usually did when standing here. In fact, Dan didn't feel anything, except numb. At least it was an improvement over the devastation that had overwhelmed him when he got the news.

How was this possible? To go from a carefree existence, to having his life shattered in the space of a few short moments.

He'd prayed hard. That it wasn't true. That it was a nightmare he'd wake up from, laugh at himself over the ridiculousness of it all, and go on with his day, knowing everything would be okay. It was a nightmare all right. But when he woke up tomorrow, it would still be there. His brother was-

Oh God, he couldn't even bring himself to say it.

He swiped at the tears that had been falling off and on all morning, and wished he could erase the memory of his mother's sobs. When she'd called to tell him, he hadn't been able to understand a word she'd said, but he remembered being scared. That he hadn't wanted to know what she was trying to say, because he knew it was going to be bad.

Then his father had taken the phone and broken the news as gently as he could. Did people really think that delivering bad news in that gentle tone would make it hurt less? Less than, say, shouting it? Or screaming it?

Dan's mother had screamed, over and over, "My baby, my baby."

His family ripped apart at the seams.

He should be doing something. Go into the office maybe. Keep busy. Except his mind didn't seem to be working quite right. When Molly and her family got here, they would all be meeting at the folk's house, but that wouldn't be for a couple more hours yet. What was he supposed to do until then?

He stared at his reflection in the window. The black slacks, white turtleneck, and tweed sports jacket he'd dressed in looked the same as when he'd gotten ready to go in to the office this morning. Those were the only things about him that looked normal. In anger, sometimes frustration, he'd run his fingers through his short dark hair so often it looked worse than when he'd crawled out of bed. His blue eyes gazed back at him, vacantly, as he continued to stare.

"Dan?"

Dan whipped around and saw his three best friends in the world standing in the dining room doorway, looking ill at ease.

"Is there anything we can do?" Cal asked quietly, moving forward and slinging a hand up to clasp his shoulder.

"You know?" Dan asked, and then shook his head at the absurdity of the question. Of course they knew. Everyone within a fifty-mile radius of Lansing knew that his brother was a murderer.

"Yeah," Jon muttered gruffly, "we heard about it on the news this morning. You okay?"

"I've been better."

"I'm sure. I'd like to say I'm surprised but..." For all that Jon cared about Dan, his longtime dislike of Bruce had never been a secret. In fact, no one had much cared for Bruce and his less than stellar lifestyle.

"What can we do?" Sam interjected, echoing Cal's earlier question. "Do you have a lawyer yet?"

"Lawyer?" Dan sneered. "Bruce deserves whatever he gets. He murdered that woman's husband." He turned back to the French doors, filled with rage. "You saw her on television. We all did. And we all felt bad for her, too. The Honeymoon Widow. My brother did that. He ruined that woman's life."

"I wouldn't say that he ruined it," Jon pointed out. "It's hard right now, but she'll get over it."

"You can be such a jerk," Cal muttered, glaring at him.

"Yeah, but you love me anyway."

"What about the lawyer?" Sam asked, pulling a chair from the table, whipping it around and straddling it. "You're going to want the best. We can kick in if you-"

"No. Thank you anyway," Dan sighed, raking a hand through his hair. "I could hire fifty lawyers if need be. But Bruce won't hear of it." His laugh was bitter. "For once in his good for nothing life, my brother has developed a conscience. He's settled for a public defense attorney because, in his words, he deserves everything he gets. And he does." Cal moved quietly to the counter, and started a fresh pot of coffee while Dan ranted on.

"How many times did I put him through rehab?" he demanded, smacking the doorframe. "How many times?"

"More than I can count," Jon said, sliding into one of the thickly padded chairs. "More times than you should have. He didn't want help, Dan. He didn't want to change. You can't blame yourself."

"I do blame myself." He cursed softly and turned to face them all. "Do you remember the day Frank Bentley was murdered? We had just closed on that property west of Lansing, and were celebrating at McGinty's? Bruce found me there, and we went outside for a while."

"I remember," Cal murmured, while Sam and Jon nodded in agreement.

"You were furious when you came back in," Jon added. "But Bruce usually manages to tick you off."

"He wanted money. A couple hundred dollars – and I wouldn't give it to him. I knew he wanted it for drugs, and I wouldn't give it to him. So he killed Frank Bentley instead."

"I don't think he actually intended to kill him," Cal reminded him. "The witness reports said things got out of control when Bentley's wife came out. It sounds like it was accidental."

"Whether he meant to or not, an innocent man is dead. If I'd just given him the money-" That memory had been haunting him since he got the call. If only-

"Don't even try to take the blame for this," Sam said, coming up out of his chair, and staring hard at Dan. "You weren't responsible for supporting Bruce's drug habit, and you sure aren't responsible because he did something stupid. The only person who can take the blame for this is Bruce."

"My head knows that," Dan said quietly. "But in my heart, I'm just as guilty as my brother."

~End of Sneak Peek~
Order your copy of The Daddy Pact by clicking below:
http://kristykjames.net/all-books/

Reviews Appreciated!

Thanks so much for reading The Secret Admirer. If you enjoyed Mark and Robin's story, I'd truly appreciate it if you'd post a short review at the store where you purchased it. I love to hear what readers think of my books. And honestly, word-of-mouth—via reviews—helps others in deciding whether to give books by indie authors like me a chance.

Thanks again!
Kristy

Other Works by Kristy K. James

Check out more books by Kristy by clicking here:
http://kristykjames.net/all-books/
The Coach's Boys Series
A Royal Sweethearts Romance Novel Series
The Casteloria Royals
The Weko Harbor Series
The Men from the Double M Series
(A Weko Harbor companion series)
The Wishes Time Travel Romance Series
As well as several standalone novels!

About the Author...

KRISTY K. JAMES'S FIRST goal in life was to work in law enforcement, until the night she called the police to check out a scary noise in her yard. Realizing that she might someday have to check out scary noises in other dark yards if she continued on that path, she turned to her other favorite love... writing. Since then, her days have been filled with being a mom and reluctant zookeeper, creating stories and looking for trouble in her kitchen.

Connect with Kristy...
http://kristykjames.net/
https://www.facebook.com/kristykjames
https://www.instagram.com/kristykjames_author/

Be sure to follow Kristy on Bookbub to get notifications for her new releases!

https://www.bookbub.com/authors/kristy-k-james

Copyright

2017 by Kristy K. James

A Personal Message from Kristy...

So I don't offend those who aren't interested, or who believe differently than I do, I'm giving fair warning so they can skip to another section of the book. Or they can just close the book and call it a day.

To those who disagree with me, I will ask that if you enjoyed the book, please don't leave a bad review because we don't share the same opinion or beliefs. Though we might not agree on spiritual matters, I do my very best to not judge others, and would ask the same of you.

Now, for those who feel like something is missing in your life, who might be frightened by what's going on in the world and wondering what happens when life on earth is over...

I believe that Jesus Christ is the Son of God. I believe that He was sent to earth to live a sinless life, to die on the cross for the sins of man (and woman), that He rose again on the third day, and now sits at the right hand of God. I also believe that He will return for those who have accepted Him as their Savior.

Why?

Because through the years, I've seen a number of miracles. Things that have no explanation except for the existence of God. And I've experienced out and out miracles for myself.

Miracles like what happened to me in 2020 (The Unluckiest Girl on the Planet?[1]). That was definitely a year full of miracles for me!

That example doesn't seem like a lot, but I want to keep this short and sweet. There are plenty more though. A near drowning, almost being

---

1.   http://kristykjames.net/2020/03/07/the-unluckiest-girl-on-the-planet/

in a head on collision at a high speed when someone in the other lane passed the car ahead of them, apparently not noticing that the car my dad was driving was *right there*. Being hit by a red-light runner who totaled my van, and being told by one doctor that I should just give up and accept that I'd never walk normally again and should just get used to wheelchairs and walkers. I didn't give up and walk just fine now.

I've also 'felt' God's presence on many occasions. That one is a little harder to explain. All I can say is when you do, you *know* it's Him.

One question people often have is if there's a God, why does He let bad things happen? Another is, why doesn't He answer everyone's prayers.

First, God didn't create the world and the people who live here to be His puppets. And second, a lot of people tend to confuse God with a genie in a bottle. A good father will love his children, discipline his children, and teach his children. But he will never give in to all of his children's wishes and demands. God is the same kind of Father to us.

Now, because I really would like to keep this short...

If any of this resonates with you and you would like to ask Jesus into your heart (what the bible calls getting saved), it's simple. You don't have to be perfect. You don't have to change who you are. You don't have to get rid of any bad habits or opinions. You don't even have to go to church. At a later time, you may want to do some – or all - of these things, but they're not required to get saved.

All you have to do is pray something like this, 'Jesus, I confess that I am a sinner, and I ask You to be my Lord and Savior. Help me to live a life that is pleasing to You.'

What should you do after that? I know I said you didn't have to go to church to get saved, but finding a good, bible-based church will help you figure out this new life you've been born in to. Keep in mind though that as with everything else in life, nothing is perfect and it may take a while to find a church that is a good fit for you.

In the meantime, here are a couple of great websites to help you on this journey. You can find the answers to many questions at the first one.

The second has bibles you can read and/or listen to for free. They have a lot of translations. My personal preferences are the NIV (New International Version) for daily reading, and the AMP (Amplified Bible) when I want to understand what I just read a little better.

https://www.gotquestions.org/prayer-of-salvation.html

https://www.biblegateway.com/

Thanks for taking the time to read this part of my book. Regardless of the decision you made, I'll be praying God's blessings for each and every one of you.

Kristy

P.S. – if you already belong to a church, I've written a couple of plays. You can get the set for .99 cents on one site, or click http://kristykjames.net/the-god-thing/ for links to stores where you can get them FREE. Just scroll about halfway down the page to get them.

Deceived

Too often in life, the choices one person makes will seal the eternal fate of others. Some of those victims will spend eternity with their Savior. The rest, sadly, will not.

In Deceived, Jill, Bob, and Alex are all offered a final chance. Will they accept the salvation Jesus bought for them at Calvary? Or will they throw away the greatest gift of all time? Because time has run out. There is a battle for their souls. The greatest liar since the beginning of time is fighting for them too.

If We Cared Enough

Being a teenager isn't easy in the twenty-first century. Being a Christian teenager is even harder. Fear of being different, of not being like everyone else, influences decisions and reactions. And they don't have the benefit of maturity or life experience either. So, sometimes, that fear keeps them from acting, even when they know what the right thing is.

If We Cared Enough presents two different scenarios. In one, teens are faced with a dilemma. Come to the defense of a bullied classmate—or look the other way and pray. In the other, another Christian overhears a conversation between a couple. The boyfriend is demanding that his girlfriend prove she loves him.

www.ingramcontent.com/pod-product-compliance
Lightning Source LLC
Chambersburg PA
CBHW021321160726
47994CB00004B/1548